The Sleeping Wall

by
Jane M. Downs

Winner of the Fiction Fix Novella Award

"Jane M. Downs' sentences refuse distance. They slip under the skin. They float in the blood stream and shiver in cartilage and the marrow of small bones. Reading them is a wondrous, trembly thing." — Mark Ari

The Sleeping Wall

Edited by Mark Ari

Editor-in-Chief	April Gray Wilder
Managing Editor	Alex Pucher
Associate Editor	Blair Romain
Copyeditor	Sarah Cotchaleovitch
Editors Emeriti	Sarah Cotchaleovitch
	Melissa Milburn
	Thelma Young

Readers

Sam Bilheimer, Brian Childers, Sarah Cotchaleovitch Krystal Davidowitz, Nicole Dominguez, Coe Douglas, Liz Flaisig, Caroline Fraley, Tim Gilmore, Laura Havice, Pam Hnyla, Laura Hyman, Kate Kaiser, Leslie Kaplan, Thomas Karst, Kris Knapp, Benjamin Liff, Robert McChargue, Melissa Milburn, Alexa Oliveras, Chrissy Rand, Sana Riaz, Heather Stafford, Brentley Stead, Thelma Straight, Nicole Sundstrom, Christine Utz, Sam Wampler, Vanessa Wells, Phillip Wenturine, Travis Wildes, Hurley Winkler

Fiction Fix

www.fictionfix.net
editor@fictionfix.net

I run along the wall, along the sleeping wall

Part One

—

Open the door. Enter the house. The child defeated by sleep. Her arm falls free of the quilt. Her mother has brushed her hair and washed her feet. The gods yearn to be earthbound. The owl's head spins on its neck. The mother sleeps. Her dreamed child remembered and unremembered. Yard of shivering birch. White dress breathless in its plastic bag.

—

1

I sit at Mother's piano, my young hands imitate her path over the keys. Like this, Medina, she'd say pointing to the correct key. The memory of her red fingernails against ivory. At her grave a wind arose from nowhere carrying the scent of tomatoes. I can smell bread baking in the oven. I am slowly growing hungry again.

Medina watches snow fall on the tips of jonquils, fill the mouths of tulips. Dissolve on Huett Lake. She blows cigarette smoke out the window. She takes off her bracelets and sets them on the sill, notices the impressions left on her wrists.

Huett Lake. Ramshackle summerhouse, sagging porches. Balsam breeze. The dock where I learn to dive. Mother kneels in the sand, scoops lake water in her hand. "Medina," she says. "Taste the water." And I lick water from her upturned palms.

In the living room James will find Medina perched on the edge of the chair. Will see her bare legs and shining hair. And beyond the window, the garden powdered with snow, the lake. He will think that spring must wait a little longer.

In spring, Father gathered iris in his arms. In autumn, he stood on the porch to follow the arc of apples falling, his hand a fan over eyes squinting into the yellow sun.

James will pace the room, touch the lamp, her books. He will resist his need to touch her. He understands that when he speaks, the spell will shatter.

At twelve I looked like Mother. "We're like sisters," she told the butcher. "Like sisters." The meat case filled with red meats, a tray of pig snouts.

The spring thaw woke James. He went to his sons, turned on the light. The one like him slept. The one like her lay on his back, awake. Turning his dark head toward his father he said, "It's the ice breaking on the lake."

Mother's closet stiff with recital dresses. Forgotten things linger in her pockets. After dinner, her music winds into us. We leave picked bones and bread crusts on our plates. How beautiful the china is when empty, scrubbed clean and shining.

Medina thinks the snow is a forgetting, a cold hand on all that aches to rise. Earlier, she watched her youngest son race over the path leading to the lake, the dog at his legs.

Mother runs the back of her hand over piano keys. What did she hear between the clicks of the metronome? See in the worn arms of chairs, in abandoned nests on porch eaves?

On the sill, a nest with dog hair, a broken glider of thin wood, a loon's egg. The jagged edge of daylight. The lake's bleak depths. Snow, white on the windowpane.

I am a twirling girl. A gyroscope-girl. I am the tap tap *of my leather shoes wheeling under the glass chandelier. Elbows hinged, my arms open and snap shut over my chest. Braids whip my face.*

2

My birth three years after Hiroshima. Perfume of April lilacs. Mother's heartbeat. The damp earth stirs. White petunias like swatches of muslin on a bleaching field. My crib white against the nursery wall.

Medina drives over gravel, her sons in the back. Rock music. Drumlins roll into forests. Spruce, maple, pine. Three blackbirds rise on oil-slick wings. She thinks her sons know nothing of love.

When in motion, Mother loves me. Back and forth over the old Persian. Her words drop onto the rug for me to collect in my apron skirt. Clock chimes. Candlelight. I know no other world. I look into the mirror, squint until I am a string of yellow light.

At dusk a nighthawk rushes over Huett, slash of white at her throat. The Old Town canoe rubs against the dock. The boys run from the moonlight.

The hidden meadow. I run past the crumbling wall, through sunflowers, warm grass. I run. Until I know only the sweet smell, the whir of insects. Until I cannot breathe.

She woke, paralyzed by a dream of a figure between her sons' beds. She'd seen the shadow that covered its face. Like a hound beneath the moon, it thrust back its head. "Philip. Michael." Their names caught in her throat. Bulbs buried in earth. All the waiting flowers.

"Tintinnabulation. Tintinnáre." Mother says. "The notes of a triad are like bells." She strikes the final note. I lean into the couch. Sound beats against my insides like a bell clapper. The furnace creaks and heat holds us.

Medina winds the clock. Springs, wheels, weights engineered so that every hour a hammer strikes a chime. *Tintinnáre.* James's shirt on a chair. She stares at the blank window. In the cupboard, wine, chocolate powder, sedatives.

Father's study. A cave of shadows and smoky scents. Book spines embossed with gilt lettering. His face lit by a single desk lamp. Milk chocolates for me in the bottom drawer beside his scotch.

3

"Here," Mother says, taking my hand. We walk through the meadow. She points and says colt's foot, shooting star, *and I repeat the names. A swallow on a branch twitches its head.*

The night before Medina left for Huett, she grabbed James's arms and wrapped them around her. Pressed her face into his neck, pulled his hand to her lips before he pushed her away.

Wind tossed leaves against the boathouse. Late summer evenings on the porch swing between my parents. The stars are alive. The sounds of the lake and my parents' breathing.

The lake's moods are a part of her. She can name fish that slip between twists of reeds, knows the loon mates for life, that its mysterious song brings rain.

At Huett, I learn to braid my hair. I wash my feet and make rosehip tea. I run through birch on a dissolving path into a receding light.

Light through birch trees. Michael's voice skims the water. Philip lifts off the dock into a perfect dive. She remembers diving from the same dock, her body rinsed and clean. Sensations of flight.

The lake rimmed in early frost. Father drapes an old sheet over the piano. I watch him secure the shutters. I don't want to return to Syracuse and school. He smiles down at me, calls me his little lapling.

She paddles the boys in the Old Town to the cove. An abandoned loon nest at shore's edge. Michael wraps the broken egg in his red kerchief, holds it on his knees. She is alone with them.

When they said Mother was dead, I didn't cry. It was cold; that's why she looked like snow. They lowered her in the ground without air or sun. She wasn't dead. In the grave, her mouth would open and sound pour out.

James's books open on the table. She doesn't fool herself that he worries about her. It's his sons he wants. With one tug, she rips the phone cord from the wall.

4

Sunday collection plates. The muted noise of coins dropped onto felt linings. Mother's face lost behind her hat's low brim. The bells of St. John's swing back and forth. A child cries. I will be a mother who speaks sweetly to her child. I will rock her in Mother's chair. I will play Brahms and other lullabies.

Mother lifts her hand to her cheek. Sheen of pearls on her gloves. Her bracelet cascades down her arm, a collision of small sounds. We rise for the benediction. Again, the bells. I think I can never know anything.

5

Before dinner Mother cuts white roses. "We share a mind," she says. She pricks her finger and laughs to see the red drop form.

Summer rain. Swarming bees, a flying carpet of brown that bristles and dips over the lawn. A dark upwelling of dropping bodies.

She smiles if I make a mistake and guides my finger to the correct key. Eyes like black glass. I lean my head against her shoulder.

Father is late. Mother will play the piano when he enters, coat thrown over his arm. She will ignore him when he kisses the place on her neck beneath her chignon and whispers her name. Ignore the sound of ice cubes dropping into his glass.

I am a girl who steps and turns a hundred times without getting dizzy. I am the vortex of my red skirt. The cut of red against white walls.

In bed, I see myself through the wrong end of a telescope. My image gets smaller and smaller until I am a black spot in a tiny round lens. The dog scratches at my door. I do not blink or move a finger.

6

Lilacs everywhere and buds broken into green. Turn the corner, cross the street. Pass the low brick wall. The closer Medina gets to home the more she is lost.

From the front steps, her mother's music streams through the open window. Discordant and rude. Notes like broken words. Notes like the sounds of enraged birds.

Up the stairs, past bookcases, cupboards, to her mother's closet. She is smaller here, dwarfed by the satin gowns fluffed out with tissue paper, held in plastic bags.

Music rises through floorboards. She opens the turquoise jewelry box. Each ring in its own slot. Earrings paired in rows. Charm bracelet coiled and still. Between the tiny harp and bell an empty loop.

Her stomach hurts. She swallows bile, slides the bracelet into the toe of a black high-heeled shoe.

The slammed bedroom door. La-la-la. Her mother sings the broken melody. Quiet as a lamb, Medina holds her breath until she thinks she will die. La-la-la. She prays for the Virgin's voice to fill her.

Through a crack in the door, she sees her mother's feet in high heels pace and pace. The phone rings and rings. Her mother steps out of her shoes. Stockings, skirt, blouse, under clothes fall to floor. She sits on the bed, pours scotch into a glass, gulps it down, pours another.

Mesmerized by her mother's nakedness, skin almost white as the sheet.

In the bathroom, water pours into the tub. La-la-la. Something taken from the medicine cabinet. Quiet, except for running water. As if the room swallowed something hollow.

Water floods the carpet in long dark tongues that creep toward her. She moves through a liquid haze, her hands and knees sinking into the wet wool.

Ladder of daylight through the blinds. She sees the shape of a snake on the wet carpet, a lamb. With each movement forward something peels away.

A blade. Her mother's head low in the water, arm outside the tub. On her hand, a red glove shines. Downstairs, the clock chimes five.

7

He knocks, sits on the empty bench. Cut iris in a crystal vase, sheets of music stacked on a table. He imagines his teacher in her blue dress, the row of buttons marching down her back. Without her, he plays scales.

He is studying Beethoven's Moonlight Sonata. He wants to make music match what he feels. Every Tuesday, lessons beside his teacher on the bench, intoxicated by the beauty of her hands, the wash of her music in which he can hear each separate note.

Upstairs a child screams. He lifts his hands. She screams again.

He finds her crouched on the bathroom floor. A skinny child, thin black braids trailing over a red sweater dotted with stars. Her face a replica of her mother's.

She clings to her mother's arm. He pries her loose. She grabs at his face. He pins her arms, releases her. She shakes her head with such violence, he holds her face between his hands to still her.

He carries her downstairs, her arms wrapped around his neck, legs around his waist like his eight-year-old sister does. "My name is James. Don't be afraid."

He is shaking now. His voice breaks. And now he sees the hallway with the brass clock, the glass *bowl beside the phone. Unlike his home, strewn with his sisters' dolls and stacking blocks, and always the sound of childish laughter or tears.*

They wait for the ambulance. He kneels and holds her hands. He thinks she is about twelve, older than he first thought. Her teeth chatter. He picks her up. The clock chimes once at a quarter past five.

"James," she whispers. Leaning back, she puts her hand over his mouth.

8

She spins through the airless house leaving a trail of rat-tat-tat. For months James still comes to practice every Tuesday. What time is it, Father? What time?

James's square nails against the ivory keys. His music a narcotic. Half asleep, she rests her head against his shoulder. Sleepy duets. Her left hand crosses over his right. It is silence that is the worst.

Sky of geese. Trailers perched on double rows of brick. They drive to his family outside Syracuse. Patches of turquoise sky spill through her. His blue-eyed sisters clap their chubby hands. And in the far meadow, pillars of bee hives.

Her dark hair loose, they stroll through fields of bronze grass. He takes her hand. She is his little sister. His heart.

Astonishing small candies wrapped in colored tin foil, all for her. He leans over the keyboard, the sonata a current that inhabits her. She touches her mouth at the opening chord. Steps dreamily over the Oriental rug. Step-turn-step-turn.

With a flourish, he brushes snow from his uniform shoulders. Where is Fort Drum? Where is Vietnam? She watches him walk down the front steps. The yard, the street, lost to white. The moon, a bone buried in sky.

At his house she saw a roan horse. Saw the tremor of its flank, the red rim of its eye.

9

The quiet library. Dusty smell of books. Just like Father's study. From the window, I see Roundy Hall and the dormitory with its skittish sounds of girls living together. Here, the world is still. Only dust spins crazy in autumn light.

Skirts must touch the floor when we kneel. We hold our books tight to our chests, sneak cigarettes behind the library.

The sunlight on the dorm also shines on our house in Syracuse. Father speaks without looking at me. Once, he touched my hair and called me Mother's name.

There are chapel bells here. They ring at 8:00 AM, noon, before dinner. At home, the bells of St. John's announce lauds, sext, and vespers. Tintinnáre. Mother's bracelet under my pillow. The tiny bell. The harp. The cross. Collision of charms. Gold, cool as the spiral of pearls in the jewelry box.

"It is the mystery of music that compels," Mother said. "The arrangement of notes makes temporary sense out of chaos. Yet it is mystery combined with order that enchants."

I watched her carve a jack-o-lantern. She was always careful with her hands slicing vegetables and meat. She wore white gloves to cut roses. White, the color of nothing.

The Sleeping Wall

Part Two

—

Look, how beautiful from above, each bomb a flower of smoke.
Look, the molten river streaming, houses paper stars in flames.

—

1

White lilies, tea cups lined up on a ledge. In Saigon, James eats bun cha. Nocturnal packs of dogs, each resembling the other. Night-children sleepily awake while others dream in beds as soldiers crowd through streets outside their doors.

A Vietnamese child, four or five, beside her elder brother. Hair like charred wood, her eyes a mineral blue. He follows them to rubble piles sprouting behind buildings. Human figures scrounging under lamplight. Broken glass, rain-glazed metal. The child squats, making herself into a teetering bowl. Her brother slaps the knuckled hands of old men, pushes past women, arms bound with rags.

James makes offerings of sliced beef, tea, cakes of rice. Creatures of stealth. She slips out of shadow, opens her hand, then backs away to hide behind her brother. Even at night, insects gather at the food.

He follows them deep into the city. They scurry like rats. Blind man's cane tapping. American music beats through a window to mix with strains of a violin from another. Thin arms, her drab dress almost white in streetlight; they stop to eat what he has given them.

She skips around the lamp post. Her brother holds an object gleaned from rubbish to light. Opening his mouth, he sings words James cannot know. Human sound fills James. An inner harmony he'd once felt as he sat beside his piano teacher, her daughter hiding somewhere in the house.

2

An old mama-san, her bowl of dust. A boy's empty tin cup.

James at the kitchen table since lunch. He will not drink his milk. He is eleven. Window of white lace. Whine of jet descending into Fort Bragg. One of the House Rules: Waste Not, Want Not.

Crates of C rations. James guards the truck, gun across his chest. The Lieutenant tosses cans into the swarm of bodies. Beans. Peaches. Applesauce. The crowd tears at each other for the food. Pears. Spam. Pudding.

He will not drink his milk. He is a crusading king waiting for his foot soldier to test for poison. He reconstructs WWII battles memorized from his father's books. He will not drink.

Jack Sprat could eat no fat, his little sister sings through the window. She chases her twin across the lawn, collapses with laughter beside her. They cover their dolls with dishtowels, sing them to sleep. They bend their heads, hair falling over their cheeks.

The crowd chases the truck. Sores on their arms, at the edges of their mouths. Hands grab onto the tailgate so hard, fingers break.

Roar of his father's '57 Olds. His mother pours the milk down the drain. Shoulder blades like axes under her cotton dress. Commander Sgt. Major. Car keys crash on counter. Kiss on her cheek. Highball. He nods at his son. Gives him a slap on the back of the head.

3

His father brews coffee, inspects their rifles. They step into the cold, cross the pasture under an opening sky. James has forgotten his gloves. His fingers ache with cold, his rifle a tube of ice. Grey dawn.

Geese overhead. The sky filled with them. Wing spans the size of a child. They fly in a V formation like B-29 Liberators.

The summer before, he ran across the pasture to the pond. A deer fled into the underbrush. That was when he was a child without a rifle. This year, he will be the one to bag the deer.

They rest their rifles against the crumbling rubble wall. His father kneels to tie a bootlace, looks up at him in easy camaraderie. James shoves his hands under his armpits. He wants to jump up and down. He has his own rifle. He wants to yell, to hear his voice vibrate through the lifting haze. He stamps his feet. A few stones tumble down the wall. One hits the trigger of his rifle. A shot tears through the silent woods into his father's arm.

4

His mother plays Beethoven on the stereo. His sisters rest their heads in her lap. He reads his father's history books. Stories of heroism, defeat, victory. Hands joined to text, he takes in what was once in his father's mind. In his closet, the German helmet, medals, a brass belt buckle.

The horses rub against the fence. Their muscles twitch without their knowing. They nuzzle sugar, their lips a whisper in his palm. Their muffled sounds at night.

Light steals over the piano hood. It has always been there, waiting. Lessons in town with the beautiful teacher. The quiet of her home. Mechanics of string, pedals, hands. Notes march across the page, the mystery underneath.

He plays for his sisters. Music floods into him. It obliterates the sound of the shot reverberating through the woodland. His memory of abandoning his father and running to the pond. Birds calling. Cold sun. He held his breath, sat on his hands, waiting for someone to find him.

The way the horses pace. He wraps his arms around their necks. Their pleasing animal odor.

5

James wakes to the gathered quiet of dawn. His stack of books, the orderly row of lead soldiers on his desk. The walls of his room. Safety. A place his father is not.

Each day he hears the gunshot ring. His father doesn't touch him anymore.

Water runs through the pipes. Footsteps heavy in the hall. His father bangs on his door, telling him to get up. Silence breaks. Steam rises from dishwater. His mother's cheeks flushed; her red hands.

After school, his mother plays her records. James at the corner desk. Clock ticking beneath a picture of a hunting scene. Music mingles with the words he reads. Analyze, memorize until the mind is drained and contentment comes. His failures buried beneath facts, theories, images—musical notes that circle around him.

In the picture, horses leap over hedges. Red coats, riding crops, black boots. A fox runs ahead of the hounds. As a small child, the scene terrified him. His father teased him for his timidity. But it wasn't fear for the fox that frightened him. It was his recognition that the fox knew he was running for his life.

His sisters build houses with cards, then knock them down. They whisper to each other.

6

James is no longer separate. He is one of a stream of green uniforms flowing from the jungle into an open field. A soldier inches forward, leaning his weight on a crooked tree limb. Others limp and twitch, sleepwalkers yanked from the shadows of the jungle like marionettes. The lifting of feet, the turning heads controlled by invisible hands. Grasses trodden.

They burned the village. Cluster of houses, chickens, dogs. Old women and men hiding. Children with bound mouths. Vines of burnt flowers.

The field fills with men until it seems the jungle cannot release more, but they keep coming, some weeping, a few carried on dirty cloth stretchers. Odors of sweat and dried blood cling to him.

An ambush avenged. A child's head wrenched sideways.

A gray sun starts its descent. Rain falls straight down between the men. Between saplings that rise straight up out of the earth and blades of thin grass. A warm rain that draws fine black lines against the sky and slips between the wooden men with their wooden faces. You can almost hear the small clicking sounds of teeth chattering in empty mouths. Their eyes seem painted on their faces, their pupils black pinholes. They don't look left or right, but down at the ground.

Night sweats. Lotus dreams. Scorched earth. Red dusk.

He has left the jungle and cannot return.

7

James sees Medina in the coltish movements of young party girls of Saigon. They have no breasts. They dart from soldier to soldier, grab at their shirts. He sees her in their obsidian eyes, narrow feet in plastic sandals and legs streaked with fine dried dust.

Velvet skin, a hungry mouth can obliterate ruin. Perfume masks air drenched with the sweat of soldiers crammed into tents. The last night the prostitute is as small as a child. Her saliva tastes of vinegar. Her red nightgown trails along the floor. He leaves accidental bruises on her arms.

The Sleeping Wall

Part Three

—

The child's paper boat on the lake. Her mother beside her. The boat grows heavy with water and stops. The child prays it will stay afloat, even though she knows it won't. If you hold a shell to your ears you can hear waves. If you hold your hands over your ears you hear your own heart beat. The boat collapses. If she listens hard enough she can hear her mother's thoughts. The way her mind grinds out words.

—

1

James's eyes are blue. The hard blue of diamonds, the blue of ice. He touches Medina and the ice melts in her hand. He holds the hair back from her face. She didn't know how empty she'd been.

She leads him to the far shore. White birch like the long spines of the dead. Stone wall. The shed damaged so long ago by fire. His hands all over her face. It is through her flesh that her heart is pierced. He could kill her and leave her there.

He whisks the sheet from her mother's piano and laughs to hear her play so out of tune. They pick blueberries that she eats from his hand. All those empty upstairs rooms. He says his sisters grew up while he was away. He says she has grown into her mother.

Bouquet of wild flowers, red wine, his college text he reads aloud. He plays Satie with the hands of a somnambulist. She dances for him with languid, silky movements. "Come here," he says. His mouth open against hers. His hand burns her thigh. Afterwards, he sweats as if he made love in a vortex of fire. They are yoked by flames. "Do you love me? Do you?"

He tries to describe the stench of Saigon pyres. Blackened faces of children. "Hush." She puts her finger to his lips.

2

Pain. Wave after wave. Breathe. One, the midwife counts. Chipped white paint on the iron bedstead. Two. Was that lightning outside? Three. James holds your ankles. Four. You are opening. You are splitting. Breathe. The midwife counts. You count.

Pain twists. Explodes. The midwife opens her black bag with scissor hands. You bear down and down. The child cuts through you. You are tearing open. You scream. You are all body. The slippery cord. An angry cry. The child in James's hands. He smiles into his son's face, throws back his head and laughs. He kisses your forehead, your mouth.

Child on your breast mewing like a kitten. You guide his rooting mouth to taste your foremilk. Warm weight. Genitals so large it seems he sprang from them. His blue eyes. You are thinning out. It is too soon to feel love. You dig your nails into James's hand.

He wraps the afterbirth in newsprint. You see him through the window, hear sounds of digging. Afterbirth buried under the old pine. The lake beyond, three-quarter moon rising. Sun falling behind the far shore hills. One last shock of blinding light. It races across the water. Shoots through the tree to glaze your arm.

3

The one like her born at dawn. Shadows gathered in his hair.

Birth. The moment is an eggshell cracking open. It all races at her. The small wet head, the stub of cord. The scraping sheet. There is no stoppage, as if she had no skin or will. As if it all could drown her. Blood glistens, smears the inside of her thighs, its scent so strong she gags. She turns into the pillow.

James at her side, the child between them. "Michael," he whispers, his breath in her hair. He traces a tear that falls down her cheek.

The child's small hand around her finger. She brings it to her mouth. Her body emptied. Her breasts ache. Outside the rain like many knives. Leaves cut from their hold.

4

Their world at Huett. Blue flowers in September. Dawn against a dusty window. Sometimes, she disappears into the trees. His classes at college. Dizzy. Bereft. Words pulse with history's stories of catastrophe, love, blindness. The meadow crossed. The broken wall. They watch constellations open over the lake.

He saw the soldier race across the field, head down, feet barely touching the ground. Someone shot him in mid-flight and then they were all around him, stripping his body down to the injured flesh.

It is the dream of Medina that captures him. The cadence of her thought, her pulse, the metronome that was her mother's. He is lost in her body. She wraps him in her hair.

Jungle dripping with heat. Vines coiled between branches. He kneels over the corpse. Hears the jungle behind him as if it were thinking, trying to speak.

Scorched village. They dig where the huts were. Broken dishes, pots, a doll, a wooden horse. Bones. The closer they get to the bones the more they swear and joke. One puts on a helmet encrusted with blood.

She collects feathers. Dead bees in a bowl. An empty mud wasp nest. Presses leaves between sheets of waxed paper. He watches her move beneath the burning autumn sky.

Memory, a movie playing frame by frame.

Broken Buddha on a fence post. A cross hung around a neck. Soldier praying inside a foxhole. A woman kneels to kiss the ground. Thunder. A couple makes love after a funeral.

5

Now, he can't stop remembering the mud and rain, everything suspended in dense light. The scorching Vietnam sun. No wind. Rows of body bags, temporary graves. How he held a cigarette to the lips of a soldier without hands. Now, he has a quiet place where he can reach into his books for answers. A place where it is possible to imagine a future. Yet, watching his sons run along the path to the lake, Medina behind them, her hair a shower of black, he wonders what they are running to.

Always restlessness, always the need to ease it. How lovely her eyes are at dusk. And the children's, too. Ice cubes gleaming in a glass. Gin cool in his mouth.

6

Winter lake. Snow. Glint of blades. Philip skates ahead. Michael's mittened hands. They are currents swept to where sleeping ducks slip their heads beneath wings on summer nights. Where fish spawn transparent eggs.

Minds overtaken by bodies, they push forward without thought of what will one day end. Snow on the bell tower of grinding wheels. Ice, pink in morning light.

7

A rusty laundry carousel. Broken clothes pins on a gray rope. She watches her sons run against the wind, shirts flattened against their chests. With a thud, Philip kicks the ball. It rises and they chase it, stomping over packed sand, hands swiping the hair blowing across their foreheads. She bites down hard on her cigarette filter. A robin breaks free from a tree.

8

Wreckage of a winter intruder. Overflowing ashtrays, hearth littered with beer bottle glass. Blood trail to cellar, delicate and brown. They find a deer on its side. She retrieves the hacksaw from the boathouse. Philip watches James from the stairs, hands over his mouth.

She stands on the dock with Michael. James and Philip paddle the Old Town to the center of the lake. Bags of deer slide overboard. Pelvis, shank, rib. It was a doe, her eyes gone to milk.

Precise reflection of birch and spruce. Her mother played scales, a slope of notes that rushed at her through trees. A loon glides in the cove, its cry stilled in the curve of its neck.

That night she will let him hurt her. He will sink his teeth into her shoulder as his life spills into her. He will find the hard knot of her nipple and suckle like an infant, his own death something not yet a possibility.

9

Medina and James make quick, hard love. It is impossible to rid her body's need of him.

I wind my music box. Inside the glass, a ballerina wheels around to carousel music, her tutu a stiff pink cloud. Her tiny perfect arm curves upward. One leg forever bends behind her. The key turns. I never let it stop.

Her eyes close and it all vanishes. She must not forget anything.

Cream-white paper stacked on Father's mahogany desk. On the chair his sweater exhales dark scents of cigar and roasted meat. A photograph taken the day he left for Europe, before his ruined leg. Tall and crisp in his army uniform, Mother's tailored white suit. Behind them, bare trees against winter sky.

Their sons are animal-like in their investigations. They love the things they trap and keep in jars. White-bellied spiders. Small cocoons. Fireflies that beat against the glass.

Inside the silver frame, Father's wide smile, the jaunty slant of hat. Mother lifts her face to gaze into his eyes. His arm protects her. His eyes adore her. The carousel music slows. I turn the key.

Yellow moon. Summer ends. Fields and orchards wait to be relieved. She hears a raccoon screech. Rain gurgles in the gutters.

The rat-tat-tat of mother's heels. Hands flutter, charms clatter. She lifts the piano hood. Her music sings inside me, and my heart races. Her music holds me, and I am inside it.

10

On the mantle a photograph. Philip beside her on the dock. Michael on her hip. The lake a shining disk between sky and earth. She missed the moment of her perfection, but the camera paid attention. The shutter opened and shut. Her image caught in the dark chamber.

11

A sea, a swarm, all the world a single mass in motion. She tries to slow it. She smokes. She drinks. She counts the clock's chimes.

She walks in the meadow where rain has bred yellow hawkweed and wild iris. Michael runs to her; a feather floats in his hand.

James plays the piano. Sounds shiver across the water. Philip at the lake's edge in his striped soccer shirt. His stone skims effortlessly over the water before it drops.

The curve of James's shoulders fills her with such longing. That first year, she went without underwear so he could have her whenever he wanted. Against the wall. On the porch floor.

His music rushes at her. A flock of birds startled from the birch. A furious sheet of rain.

She grabs hold of her chair, as if the flood would lift her. The play of hammer and string. The balance of melody against everything else.

And they are all caught up in the resonance—as if there was no other world outside of it, only the lake and the gathering smell of rain.

The canoe. The lake a mouth. She was careless with what she loved. It was always too much. Wild geese always calling, cupboards needing to be filled. The children watch the metallic clouds move above the lake. The water turns black.

Part Four

—

The child wakes. The mobile over her crib. Little white lambs circle with no-where to go. Round and round. Hypnotic. The door creaks open. She's figured this out—door opens and she will be touched. Right now, she knows only the hands of her mother, her father. Gentle hands. Right now it is magic opening. All of it.

—

1

James is late for his class. Mai is without an umbrella. He holds the door. She brushes against him. Rain beads on blue-black hair.

Medina at the edge of his vision. Spinning woman. Spinning world. Bracelets clatter. Scented lipstick. His sons run across the meadow, shirts flapping like flags in wind.

Mai in the front row. He hands out the syllabus. Her feet are wet. He starts with Hegel. She takes notes in a small black notebook.

Her back toward the house, Medina sits for hours at the dock end. Lost in a book. Lost in a dream. Lost to them all. The boys in an attic room devising codes. Whittling with their new knives. She calls their names; her voice melts into the lake.

Yes, I was in Saigon. We lived on rue des Lille. They destroyed me then they saved me.

Empty wine bottles. Medina's mark on everything. Hair like ravens. He catches her arm. She spins away. They paddle the Old Town to the far shore. She takes him into her. *Open me. Make me feel. Make me feel.*

Mai makes him tea in her celadon teapot. Gibbous moon. She feeds him almonds. A plate of oranges. Waning crescent moon. She is obsessed with hummingbirds.

One night a syzygy. Moon, earth, sun clumsily aligned.

2

James's desire for Mai stuns him. Her clipped, precise English, handwriting careful as a schoolgirl's. Caught in window sun, she seems a chrysalis encased in light. When she walked into his classroom he hadn't known an instant could transform him so completely.

Again and again, he goes to her as if in a dream where he is without will. Her room holds such stillness—a boat adrift in the middle of a lake. Air tinged with the closed-up scent of secondhand books that line her walls. Her soft hands clutch the sheet. Before he leaves, she tiptoes to press her lips against his eyelids.

3

Mai's world lost piece by piece. There is a rhythm to the losing. The way purple herons lift and lower their heads, their spindle legs vanishing in tall grass.

Saigon, city of bones, rises in smoke. The sky bends down to meet it. The stripping away until things reveal themselves as without weight. Without roots.

The Mekong is a molten river, bridges fingers of flame. She watches her mother bury the polished Buddha under bamboo leaves. She feels a sudden pain, her heart fighting against its own death.

The darkness is a ruin. Her mother's hand, twigs of bone in hers. More refugees, tense links in a chain of bobbing lights. Footprints dissolve as if in sand.

Boatmen lean against lampposts smoking. Those who would try to break her open. Rough and careless, not like she imagined her father in his French army uniform. She pieced him together from a torn image in black and white. He visits her dreams offering oval pebbles piled in a rice bowl. He left her his name, left her his language ma fille, mon amour.

Boats, ribbed cradles anchored in red morning. She stares at the lapping water, vessels battered by the sea. Her teenage body. She lifts her chin, straightens her spine and faces the eastern glare.

Her mother unbraids her hair, combs it with her fingers. Her mother sighs. Wind howls through their ribs.

4

Always, something simple arouses him. Strand of hair across Mai's cheek, curve of ear lobe. He pushes up against what at first seems impenetrable. Kisses her eyes, peels away her clothing. She opens under his hands, admits him to her very center.

Black storm. We crowd under the tarp. Maman shivers and I rub her arms. Rain like bullets. Swell after swell, the boat listing, us listing with it. Nothing connects to anything on the sea. The endless sea.

Bodies joined, he feels her yield, imagines an emptiness, into which he will pour himself.

Her center a vast hollow where thought and memory perish. All is acquiescence. He is hostage to this simple truth.

Maman smells of fever, her thirst inhuman. We huddle together. I recite poetry memorized in school. Words I thought I'd forgotten speak themselves through me to maman.

Pour inviter les oiseaux du reve au chevet.

He bathes her, sponges between her small toes. Her scars intrigue him. He traces the long glossy one that trails over her arm. Studies the splatter of white pinpoints on her skin.

"Speak in my tongue, Mai," Maman says, her voice almost lost.
may theo chim ve day nui xa xanh tung.

Here is where they stitched me. Here is where the shrapnel was extracted.

I rub Maman's feet, press her head against my chest. Others pull her away. She slides into the ocean. I see the rain is made of tears. The outlines of a great bird rise inside the storm. Wings shudder open and close. It holds my life in its talons, my words in its beak.

He folds her in her robe, reads a lesson while she rests in his arms. Searches her eyes for signs of resistance, his face twinned in the dark pools.

Buddhists burn their dead, release the ashes into wind. The dead never go away. The dead are everywhere.

She is tired. She listens to him close the door. From Saigon, to the Philippines, L.A., New York. No one left to run to. She accepts this place of spruce and snow. Birch like mist twisting up from rice fields. She is grateful for her scholarship. For this man with ice-blue eyes who tries to heal them both with his hands.

5

Medina accuses James of not loving her. Of trying to hurt her. Her flushed face. Her mouth stretched tight, stained with wine.

He can't tell her of Mai, who writes poems in black notebooks. That he is overwhelmed by a submission to all he had buried after the war.

She accuses him of not loving her. Of avoiding her. He begins to pace. She grabs his arm. "Stop. Look at me. Touch me." Her elbow sends a glass crashing to the floor.

He can't tell her he is unraveling thread by thread. Of Mai whose body gives reprieve. Whose room holds a brass Buddha polished by candle light.

He leads her to the piano, covers her hands with his own. Directs them to play familiar patterns. She softens beside him. She weeps. He kisses her mouth.

"You are my life. Our sons are my life." Lying beside her, he strokes her. She comes in long waves. She cries out. He holds his hand against her mouth. He knows he is falling away. It is the vanishing that betrays her.

6

Silhouette of birch. Early birdsong. A child's fort built of branches and leaves. Children's footprints in the sandy grass. Medina wraps herself in her wool shawl, watches her sons fight with sticks thin as switches. "En garde." Philip advances. Michael retreats. Hiss of sticks. The dog jumps and snaps. Imagined wounds.

She holds out her hand for their weapons. Philip throws his at her feet, salutes and turns away. She does not see the child, only his anger. She grabs his arm. He wrenches loose to disappear into the fort, a house too fragile to hold him.

7

Mai is ravenous. He feeds her books. Nietzsche, Hume, Freud underlined and full of marginalia. He drinks gin he keeps in her cupboard. Argues truth is philosophical, that artists are the architects of cultural heritage. He sees death everywhere, says we create artifice in order to not be swallowed by it.

He speaks of his family as if they are from another century, his sons not marked by his own fate. Mai knows he will never leave them. His sons are mirrors. He talks of walking with his wife in fields beyond his family home before the war.

She takes what he can give. Above all things, she is practical. That is enough for now.

He speaks of Vietnam; she listens. He holds his head between his hands. He cannot stop himself from talking. He paces her room, tapping his fingers on every surface.

She chooses images: Saigon's boulevards clogged with cars and bicycles. Whirl of saffron robes, girls teetering on gold lame shoes. Markets where shackled chickens squawk and plumed birds dart from perch to perch in bamboo cages. She inhales incense, jasmine, human excrement and sweat. Every hour the sound of church bells wash alleys and rooftops clean.

The nuns cried when they kissed her goodbye. She sees herself, neat in her navy blue school uniform, her pigtail straight down her back, her dreams inside her like fragile glass.

The war. Funnel of wind. Horizon of flames. Children open empty hands. Sun on a face, then blood.

Later, he pounds his body into hers. She craves the harshness of it. As if her listening deserves punishment, her acquiescence penance for her survival when so many died. She knows he will bathe and stroke her. He will cradle her and, for a while, she will be all body. He will leave her books to set on shelves she made from cinder blocks and plywood.

Her name on his lips, his voice inside her. She hoards his words for poems she writes in black notebooks with blue-lined paper. Vietnamese, French, English. At times, she thinks she will become deranged by words. Each new language a transparent skin pulled tight over the skeletons of the others. Each new poem something ripped from both of them.

Long hours bent over books in her rented room the size of the one she'd shared with Maman. She heats up tom yum soup, imagining Maman reading in the corner, her book lit by a kerosene lamp. Mai writes.

Part Five

—

The child's room is a box. Three dolls akimbo on the sill. Door without a lock. She pleats their skirts and combs their hair. Wraps lace around their wrists. She is the maker of dreams. She is the taker of dreams. She is the guardian of lost dolls.

—

1

Milk poured into little pitchers, then set on the table. Vine bent along the fence, twig on the back step. Shoes piled in the hallway. A horse fly has bitten Michael's arms. Medina opens a book. Mold splatters the pages.

Noon sunshine. Nowhere to hide. The boys doze in the rope web of the porch hammock. She lines up their shoes. Pours water into potted geraniums. Blue sky falling through branches. The Old Town needs varnish. Unmade beds wait.

She thinks she is trapped in a story. How can she know what she thinks? Behind pale blue eyelids, Michael's eyes roll into his head. He seems abnormal, alien.

Last night, she and James lay in bed not touching or speaking, knowing the other awake, the silence between them thick gauze. She said his name. The clock's chimes surged through her. Molten silver. *Tintinnáre.*

A hawk flies over Huett. Its cry rolls over the water, fades into the horizon. Her thoughts shift like light on waves. She longs for winter's breath on her face. Stillness of snow. Sound of ice on leaves, reeds glimmering swords.

She rocks the hammock. Philip's eyes snap open. A black bird crows, then another and another until the tree screams.

2

A glass of milk slides through Michael's hands. Shattered glass in a pool of white.

James had said, We make our own history. We make choices. She pulls his shirt around her, slides his hunting knife into her jeans.

Mother's hands come down hard on ivory keys. Eyes closed, she leans into the piano. I sink into my chair, mouth words to made-up songs. Chair, piano, even Mother, are made of sound. Things I can put my hand through.

Drawers of mismatched silverware, unused marrow spoons. She grabs a corkscrew. The foil over the bottle top slices her finger. Blood on a plate. Blood on his shirt. Tap water of rust. Her bracelets clang against porcelain. Spring snow falls through birch. Snow melts into the lake.

Cattails and lily pads. I float, my unbound hair flowing around me. I dive to the bottom in search of fronds in the dim green. I dive to where light fades and my fingers turn cold. Even here, the current a kind of music.

Window fogged by steam. Hot dog water thick with fleshy scum. Philip's eyes the sharp tips of daggers. Michael's rabbity bites. Red wine hot in her throat. With the tip of her cigarette she lights another. Pour another glass. Another glass.

Mother's eyes veined yellow by lamplight, my face between her hands. Music records history, she says; you learn what was forbidden, for that is where the music comes from. A wisp of hair floats over her forehead. I dare not touch it.

Bitter wine. Sunset. No wind. With snow, a sudden chill as if the day's heat was an accident. She runs to the boathouse, trails her hand over the Old Town's wooden gunnels. She looks at her hands, broken lifelines on both palms.

3

At the window she sees headlights, but it is the last of daylight clinging to birch. Her hand flat against the window. Her wine tastes ripe, dark. Dusk. Stars nailed to sky.

His absence carves a pit into her stomach. She fills her glass, lifts it to the light. Red liquid aglow with rash radiance.

Her insides are heavy. She thought his love was perfect. Another drink. Abeyance is the word she works hard to remember. She is set aside, suspended.

The pit in her opens and opens until she is hollowed out. Except for the warmth of the wine spreading, seeping through her. Wind moves through branches in such lovely rhythm. Measured beats of waves fold over the shore. She must go to the lake.

James will come. He will charge through the empty house, his voice echo through its rooms. Pain splinters through her head. Stars' bleak shards. A terrible noise inside her head. Glass breaking. The lake dilutes memory. The way the Old Town embraces you.

4

Stack the wood. Start the fire. Boys, be quiet. More wine. Another cigarette. She can't sit still. B flat is off. She can't get the notes right. Outside, jonquils receive late snow. The dog spins and spins after its tail. Be still.

I run to find the sun, but it's been stolen by slate clouds the color of a junco's wings. The road cuts fields burnt by summer. Wires burdened with birds. The silence grows louder. Except for the breaking of leaves underfoot. Except for my panting.

Michael raises his arms as she pulls on his jacket. Philip's feet stamp stamp. Two pillows, two blankets carried to the Old Town. Thermos of hot chocolate. White moonlight drains the blond from Philip's hair, turns his hands blue.

On hands and knees I make a house of sticks to fill with dead grass and dry clover. Reek of sulfur before smoke. Quick heat on my face. The house explodes into flames. Time is still.

Boys head-to-toe in the Old Town. Film of snow on the gunnels. Michael's raised hand, delicate as a reed. They all know the melody. They hum what she couldn't play. Her head swims. Glare of moon. Children of light.

Flame, clean like water. Again, I am running. Away from the parched field, the thin trail of smoke. Back to Father and Huett. To bury my face in the dog's fur.

Lift and pull of paddle. Wind at their backs. A raccoon's churring knifes through her. The boys pass the thermos. She watched James kneel between their beds, a supplicant. He touched their foreheads and they stirred in sleep.

Mother always held my hand. I remember that one thing most. Walking through fields, the distant line of drumlins changing color with the light. My hand warm in hers. The rustle of her skirts.

The wind ceases. Cold stills them. Philip's red mittens. Michael's scarf wrapped round and round. Wine in a flask. Night washes over them. The canoe, for a moment, motionless, hangs on time. Fish numbed by winter's last breath. Limb of birch, blind sentinels.

5

His hands on the steering wheel. Past the crossroads, moss-patched houses. Porches strewn with pine needles. Snow on the windshield, the highway hurtling toward the horizon. Taste of Mai. Dim light spreads over sloping hills. Snowflakes spiral.

Huett's water raked by wind. The untouched piano. Medina's musky scent on every surface. Her hair black orchids or ravens. He can't bear to touch her. He can't bear not to touch her. Mornings, he wakes like a crazy man.

Left onto Route 9, past fields cold in the encroaching dark. He searches the glove box for a tape hidden behind wadded Kleenex, a child's plastic gun. Mai had turned, exposing the thin skin of her neck. He'd filled her mouth with his fingers.

The iron bed with chipped white paint. Medina's bracelets on the dresser, cold silver reflections in the mirror. Her way of lifting her hair exposing a web of veins pulsing at her temples.

At the crossroads, an animal's eyes, ovals of hard reflected light. His secret life is an affliction. His students look at him with open mouths. He takes comfort from nothing. Only his sons. Only Mai who smells of plums.

An owl sweeps over the road. He thinks of his sons running, always running, through forests of birch. Appearing, disappearing behind white columns. Flickering children in a movie that spins round on a reel.

Medina at the end of the dock, a child on either side. They turn toward him. Wall of water. The horizon. Molten metal below. Above, falling fire.

He punches in the tape. Music explodes, then settles into a familiar strain that relaxes him, propels him through the delicate snowfall. He will climb steps strewn with shoes and small sailboats. He will gather his sons to him, breathe in their salty scents, feel the small, tight muscles of their backs.

6

The landscape stiff with cold. Without James you are in pieces. The wine makes you clumsy. You see yourself and your sons as the nighthawk would: a torn branch floating on the lake.

James said that when he set off a round of ammunition, he released pieces of himself. He said he was lodged inside each human being he'd killed.

The cove. The far shore where you first drank from his body. He kept touching your face. And now, you are crying. You turn toward the house. Light flickers through birch. Two cones of light on the lawn. You stand up and call his name, your voice a flame. The Old Town rocks. Philip yells, "Sit down!"

He pulls at your shirt, and you jerk away. The Old Town lurches onto its side. You aren't able to stop them from falling. You follow.

Water rushes into your ears and mouth. You cannot see or think. The paralyzing cold steals your strength. You struggle to the surface. A hand grabs your hair, drags you down. You pull the weight against you. It thrashes away.

Michael's head bobbing near the Old Town. You grab his arm. He clings to you. He gags and spits. You cannot feel your body. Your wet clothes pull you down and down. Your lungs burn.

You hear Philip splashing. He swims away from you toward the lit windows of the house. You know you have only minutes before the cold completely drains you. You reach for him again and again. He's beyond your grasp, arms flailing, head jerking from side to side.

Michael's chattering teeth against your throat, his jaw working as if unhinged. You plow through the water to the shore where you sit, Michael cradled in your arms. His eyes click open and shut. He is choking.

You fumble for James's knife, your hands blunt, without fingers. With your teeth you cut the ties of his jacket that have tangled around his neck. He gasps, his skin like cold rubber. He reaches to touch your hair.

A cloud swallows then releases the moon. "Mommy, mommy," Philip calls. You strain to see him. Shadows leap out, collide into each other as the dark gathers around him. You are paralyzed by cold, by the breathing weight in your lap. You cannot make your hands work or move your legs. Your teeth rattle, and your mouth forms his name, your voice frozen deep inside you. You hear him splash, then only silence.

7

The snow never stopped. Gray clouds pasted to the sky. Rescue boat, its light smearing birch with red. He was given two sons. Now, he has one.

Upstairs, you rub Michael's hands between yours. He doesn't speak. You are afraid to let him sleep. You lie beside him, and when he closes his eyes the dark thickens around you.

James wakes to the cries of geese flying north. Their long black necks, their beating wings. Cold sun rising, behind it the dream unremembered. He cannot think about what is lost.

The sedative wears off and you can hear your every heartbeat. You hear your blood surge through your arteries. You rock in your mother's chair and gaze at Huett, Michael on the rug beside you, his shoulder against your leg. Always, he is near you, touching you. The clock strikes twelve. The sound almost unbearable. Twelve chimes inside your skull. Tintinnáre.

8

Saint Anne's cemetery. Black wrought iron gate. Muffled voices. A crow flies past the granite headstone, beyond bird-lined wires and clouds and the blue that grows whiter and thinner until it isn't blue anymore. Until it isn't anything anymore.

You sleep. You wake. You slip back into a dream of gentle happiness. Your mother brushes your hair with a silver-backed brush, divides it into two plaits. Huett gleams like quartz. Trees drawn black against it, as if a pen had sketched them.

She didn't know the world she created would be a replica of the one she fled.

Your mother and father on the dock, you between them. Soft breeze in trees. Emerald world.

Run to the field. Taste the dew. A snake parts the grass. Its cool body grazes your leg.

A gust sweeps through Saint Anne's. Lilac air. Noon sun. She sweats beneath her dress. James holds her elbow, her weight against his arm. Michael's hand in hers.

The sun rises even if you want the night to last. You lift your face to warmth even as you crave the dark. You sleep. You rise, your dreams like tissue dissolving.

They turn to leave. Church bells call for mid-day prayer. Sound carves shapes out of fields. Sound, a membrane tight around her head. Charms, dumb at her wrist.

9

He understands the spell is broken. Black crow glistening at the grave. Tree branches knuckled with buds. Tips of flowers thrust upward in search of light.

The soldier in Saigon without hands, the corpse on Ho Chi Minh Trail. Now, he is one of them.

Medina in the rocker. Michael on the dock, the dog in his arms. James puts his hands on her shoulders. His touch crosses her flesh into ice.

Spring unfurls itself, an assault. Birch drip with seeds. No one sleeps. The loons return, their cries like sobs. No one speaks of her carelessness. Of Mai. Waves slap the dock.

Perhaps, he can only love what he holds in his mind—voices of the past in endless argument, searching for resolutions that elude them. Each day he falls further away from hope, from the fable of redemption.

Their sons had raced around her. She'd held up her wrists to show him her bracelets.

10

Gin in a glass. He plays *Moonlight Sonata*. He is a boy beside his teacher, inhaling her perfume. His mother at home washing his sisters' dresses. Soft clattering of dishes. The slow sounds of horses in the field.

She dreams she rises like a spirit above the bed. Something unformed, without sensation, con-

tained by the vaulted ceiling, spreading out until she fills the space. Her sleeping body a brittle locust shell. Within its crust a void.

The clock's hollow chimes. Gin burns his throat. His mind goes blank. Fumbling, his hands remember. Music moves through him like his own blood. Pieces from the *Fifth Symphony*. Beethoven's great despair.

She dreams a bridge between lake and house. A dreamed bridge for a dreamed child.

11

Fields of unbound hay. Lichen feverish against black trees that clutch the shore. What is that sound? Spirits cling to the birch, each shape without a face. Without feet. Your emptiness. Huett is luminous, your heart black. You grip the chair, Michael's hand. The soles of your feet are unclean.

You know what your Mother heard between the clicks of the metronome. Catastrophe within. The silence that binds everything together. Your knowledge is without words. It is like a heart folding in upon itself.

The owl lifts from the tree, muscled wings and feathered heartbeat. Your hands are always cold. Dead sun. Hoarfrost. Night sweats. Huett receives its own darkness.

12

The night they found the deer in the basement Michael asked, *Daddy, what happens when you die?*

Your soul goes to heaven.

How do you know it goes to heaven if you can't see it?

Your soul is like the wind. You can't see it, but you can feel it.

James blew into Michael's upturned palm. Michael drifted into sleep.

13

Mai misses his touch. He said her scars were places where the world knifed into her. Pieces of it beating inside her, trapped by silvered skin.

Memory seizes her. All else a flimsy overlay.

Flares against night. Starched scent of her white communion dress. Flocks of red-billed babblers dipping over the old French road.

A spider spins a thread in lamplight. From her bookshelves, voices break into her room, each one torn from a different past. She fears she will die before she has made them her own. Before she has rid herself of her remembered world in order to create a new one.

Saigon morning. Buddhist monk. Smell of gasoline, then the match. That moment when fire holds the kneeling skeleton. One last embrace before it turns to ash.

Red sunrise. Sheets of rain. The clock's hands freeze, its pendulum a silent needle. Bound white paper on her desk. She lifts her pen.

14

Michael holds a blue egg wrapped in a kerchief. You kneel to receive it. It is beautiful, complete. The shell a wall between your hand and unformed life.

Soon the nighthawk will build its home of twigs and grass. Loons circle their nest with flapping wings. One will stop to stare into the sun.

15

His axe rises and crashes down on the Old Town. Torn canvas. Wood chips flying. Until his arms are too weak to lift. She steps in from the boathouse door and takes the axe. Their fingers touch. They stare into each other's eyes, the axe dangling from her hand.

The Sleeping Wall

Part Six

—

Her mother leans into the piano. Music floats in apple trees. It falls around the child. She is carried to bed. She is unable to resist the close of day, protest its brevity. She has been bathed in music. It is what gathers in her mind as she drifts somewhere other than the world she tries to know.

—

1

All the light is shattered. The dog licks my hand. I can't wake up.

Phone calls. Inquest. She waited for James to come to her. Bedrooms filled with aunts, cousins, uncles. James at the dock in his suit. The blue veins at Michael's temples.

I've cleaned the house. Beaten the rugs. Stripped the walls bare, scrubbed them. Emptied cupboards, drawers, bookcases. Boxes overflow onto the porch. My hands are raw. I'm always cold.

She waited for James. He played the piano. Gone for hours. Plates of untouched food. He carried Michael to bed.

I paint the kitchen, dining room, living room. Paint over smoke stains on the hearth. Clean windows with newspaper. Strip beds. Burn photographs and letters.

A woman brought her tea, made her hot soup. She answered the phone.

My dresses are clean. They sway on the rope.

2

She tells him to take whatever he wants. She watches, smoking while she leans against the wall. Every movement an injury. Clothing in boxes. Books. A stack of sheet music. Philip's things. They are all a little dead.

In the hammock, a child on either side. Sky the color of pearls. Blueberries tasting of summer rain. Shoulders pink from sun. James bounds up the steps.

He leaves a razor on the sink. Dirty clothes in the hamper. A bottle of gin in a drawer. Part of her relishes his pain. She knows if he stayed she would always see Philip, feel his anger. To lose Michael would have killed her. She is desperate. She would do anything to heal them.

She can't eat. Can't sleep. Can't think. She wanders into a room and Philip is shooting marbles, brushing the dog, stacking wood. He is diving, floating, skipping stones. He is eating, singing, bathing, crying, catching a ball.

Back and forth over the old Persian. Her sons collect her words in their pockets. They grab hold of her skirt with their fists.

3

James packs the car. Before they leave, Michael tosses a stone into the lake. The dog dives, comes up empty-mouthed. The lake has eaten the end of the dock. A human soul can endure anything.

The first of May we weave baskets to hang on doors. Tie tulips and jonquils with ribbon. In the meadow, Mother's skirts flying. I am everywhere, carried by wind, my flesh and bones blown high like milkweed seeds.

Wild geese huddle on the far shore; their heads turn on long black necks. She crushes balsam in her hand. Michael bends to inhale the fragrance, his lips against her palm. Blank-eyed Michael. Silent child.

On our backs in the meadow. The sky an empty screen where anything can be imagined.

They stood over Philip, failed sentinels.

At the dock, Mother says, Perch, sunfish, bass. She points out a cloud, and I say, Cirrus. Her hair lake-shine and sun. You can touch water. You can't touch light.

Those first days without them. White feathers scattered over wet sand. Two beds side-by-side. Two bicycles against the boathouse. Her reflection in the night window. There are bones in the walls.

4

Medina's cigarette smoke twists and vanishes. The nighthawk sweeps low over Huett, her brown wings point skyward. Medina sleeps. She wakes. She knows she cannot leave this dream.

Summer ends. Tall dry flower stalks bent at edge of lawn. The lake rids itself of birds and heat. Yellow leaves cling to birch. She always rubs her hands together, wipes her hair from her face. If James returned she would not let him touch her. She would break.

Each day at Philip's grave with offerings. A clutch of yarrow ripped from the yard. Bread wrapped in her scarf, two cat's-eye marbles in a cup. She lies on the sun-burnt grass. Knots of weed in the packed earth.

Stunned, she let her weight fall against James as the casket was lowered. Cascading earth like gravel striking the polished wood.

She sleeps. She wakes. Falling from one world into another, shedding one self for another, slipping out of sun into falling dark. She dreams of foxglove spotted with dew, light caught in a porcelain bowl, spiders that furiously wrap the house in webs. Images rise and fall like the clock pendulum inside its glass case.

5

His guilt waits for him. He cannot wear it yet. It is slippery, moving in and out of his mind. It is unclean skin.

Insects in the air, tumbling. They climb down the slope into the summer meadow. Blue bells, tiny snapdragon, balls of dandelion seeds. Mai's hot from their walk. She takes off her shirt. A breeze bends the tall grass. He lies beside her. Her flat belly. Pulse in her throat. Dappled light on her face.

Her seriousness moves him. She must find meaning in everything. The efficiency of her hands as they write or prepare food. Sometimes, just the sight of her hands.

A box of Philip's things. How little he owned. Two jackets, the tiger's eye, frayed baseball cards he'd put on his bicycle spokes.

The only sound is from the breeze. Slits of sunlight through pearl-gray clouds. Her shadow tilts in the grass. A shaft of heat runs through him.

He answered the phone. She'd read about it in the paper. All he heard was her crying.

6

Mai walks the ridge along the fieldstone wall. Snarls of ivy. Tick of switch she drags over the rough surface. Wind-seized smoke of burning leaves. Isles of maples, furies of orange and red.

The old French road on which we flee. Maman's soft footfall, her short breaths. Wall of river rock blanched by moonlight. Endless wall.

She is no longer held. She misses that. His hot breath, hands exploring her as if he would find something hidden from them both.

Uneven surface of stones. The waterfall behind it. Our listing shadows.

He calls at midnight; the ringing calls her back to Saigon nights swollen with the swing of church bells, their tongues loosely falling back and forth. She stares at the phone. Her heart in its cage. Her white nightgown. Phantom bride.

Streetlight etches spines of books she will take with her to Boston. James said, We must serve death by remembering. He kissed her eyes.

Night collapses. The wall rises out of the dewed earth in new light. Where it is broken, shards of bottle glass, wads of paper, an extravagance of white jasmine.

7

Medina stands from kneeling at Philip's grave. A woman on the near slope, watching.

Blue-black hills. Battered sky. The dog shivers in the dawn cold.

The ground where Philip rests not yet part of the earth but suspended within it. At first she thinks the woman is a girl. They both wear red. Both stand straight. Medina's black hair loose, the other's tightly braided.

Medina forms a frame with her hands through which to view the woman. The long distance between them. Did she see the woman cross herself?

The dog runs around her in circles. She calls his name and bends to stroke his head. She looks up. The woman is gone, the wind a broken chord.

8

Translations in Mai's careful script. Words measured, weighed. Huy Can's *dream birds flock 'round a bedside.* Bich Khe's world of *velvet clouds, ethereal hands.*

Flocks of words, each one a respite from loneliness. French. Vietnamese. English. She runs along the wall of history, her thoughts the offspring of her union with another's mind.

Trees sleep in final blaze. Birch empty themselves of copper leaves. First thorns of frost on the pane. Gathering quiet something soft she can rest her head on. Something that could smother her.

9

Sky marbled gray over the Charles River. Again, displaced. With each move towards home Mai moves farther away from one. Words are her harbor. The music of history forged into shapes, distilled into sound. Talismans that keep her safe.

Her rooms fill with objects that have found her. Ivory goddess. Thin bracelet of glass beads, second-hand volumes of books. Anchors for her new life. Her body reclaimed. Flesh no longer a balm, a salve spilling through James's fingers.

Beyond her window, steeples pierce the city sky. Sway of church bells, scintilla of sound from another world. She closes her eyes. Sees herself running past the old French wall, her jacket a splash of crimson against a crumbling surface, her long braid an arrow down her back. She runs and runs until she disappears.

10

Michael. Stilled child. His shuttered mouth. He shakes his head but will not speak.

Darkening walls. James holds his child to him. Each small path forward dissolves.

Night of drunken love, Michael in the doorway. Medina's raised legs, his back an arch. James slammed his fist against the wall, stayed inside her until he came.

Their upstairs flat wrapped in an elm's weathered arms, fringed in night. Each afraid to lose sight of the other. Wasp nest brittle in eaves. Michael's box—blue egg, the dog's front tooth, a wooden ball.

If he hadn't known the boiling heat of Vietnam. Saigon filth wiped clean by a woman's hand. The way Mai lowered her head when lost in thought. How that one gesture offered such desperate comfort.

Stacks of books. Gin bottle on the table. Michael's yellow sweater. Color of a crossing guard's belt. Philip's death waiting to be folded into memory.

11

Michael beside James. An open book. Wings of leaves against the pane.

He led Medina to fields beyond his home. Grass raked by wind, jerking heads of flowers. She raced before him. Raced and spun in sunlight, hair a black stream. His image in her eyes, encircled by shining dark. He loved most what was in her that he couldn't know.

James studies Michael. The thinness of him. Girlish mouth. String of vertebrae. Ribs. Hands delicate, half moons rising on bitten nails.

His blue-eyed sisters rode the roan horse bareback, their fleshy thighs tight around its sides. His home filled with dolls and unwashed cups. His mother's high-pitched voice calling their names.

He buys a piano. Opens the window. They sit on the narrow bench. Beauty of the treble clef. Black notes leap across lined pages, flash against white. He plays a simple chord from Brahms. Michael imitates. He drapes his arm across Michael's shoulder. Michael leans into him. Outside, the weather-beaten tree. Inside, music curves, caresses.

The wet field. Lilac air. She turned in widening circles. Wild iris. The broken stems of violets.

12

Drink the wine. Wind the clock. She stripped each room bare as the inside of winter. Yet, they are everywhere. Philips's mouth stained with blackberries. Michael's flat shadow on the wall. James's hands opened over piano keys.

How lovely when she touched them, warm skin yielding beneath her hand.

The dream about pulling Philip out of the lake, dressing him in warm clothes. The dream where he runs through the house calling for her. Crazy patterns on the floor.

She sees them in the Old Town. She sits in the bow, James in the stern, the boys bundled between them. Each stroke a measure. Lift and pull. Beat after beat.

Winter's violence approaches on the feathered wings of geese. The cold slows the lake. She cannot describe it. Something at the horizon's edge. Cold light falling. She closes her eyes. She wants to be numb.

13

The clock's chimes wake her. Empty beds. His closet door ajar. Bare wire hangers. Her mind choked with memories.

Haunted birch. Candlelight. Lilacs everywhere. They waded beyond the dock. She floated in his arms. They danced in the water, toes dipping into the sand. Her hair wet against her shoulders.

She knows every bend of shoreline, every plant and tree. She draws a map in her mind. Counts trees. Traces pathways to hidden nests. She knows where bats retreat at dawn.

Cut iris in a crystal vase. Pearls on white gloves. The bells of Saint John's. She saw a roan horse. Its red-rimmed eye. Birch like the spines of the dead. The iron taste of lake water. Forgotten things in pockets.

She thinks she can imagine almost anything. The meadow a sea of green. Her sons racing ahead. Flowers that open only at night. A moving sky. She should have dropped to her knees.

14

From her window, the birch forms a tangle of arms washed with moonlight, flowers beneath it tiny gravestones. She slips out of herself. Flees into the yard to climb the tree toward the hard, round light she once knew but now cannot name.

Hand over hand, she pulls her airy weight through night and bits of light. She twists and writhes and settles on a branch. Exhausted, nervous, afraid of falling.

How she mourns the rush of blood, flesh that warms the bone. But she knows longing is never enough. The tree asserts its claim, pulls her into its sooty bark. Moonlight a river, indifferent, blind.

Night erases the house. Except the circle of light reflected in the window. Hint of face and hand as if an x-ray.

15

She burns her mother's music

Sheet after sheet into the fire

The paper devours itself

16

Medina rocks in her mother's chair. Lines of lead divide the window, break lake and birch into pieces different from what she remembers. One morning, ice will lace lake to shore.

The sky is blue. The lake the color of Philip's eyes before they closed them. Michael, my own child with midnight eyes.

Arc of the clock's brass pendulum. Its minute hand drags, then pulls forward with a snap. Call of nighthawk passing low, her speckled eggs unguarded at roof's edge.

Beyond memory stands a wall of forgetfulness. The wall is white. Behind it, you can hear grass pushing through earth, the rustle of your mother's skirts. You can hear your own death.

Her heart holds ruin. Her bracelets cut into her wrists, the blue veins there. Piano keys under their wooden hood. The minutes of her life notes of a fugue. She turns from the sun's glare.

17

Mother kneels at my bedside, her hand hesitant above me. Her bracelet slips over the small bones of her wrist. Charms polished, at rest. One cold against my forehead, another a pinprick on my cheek. If we could stay here forever.

www.ingramcontent.com/pod-product-compliance
Lightning Source LLC
Chambersburg PA
CBHW050914120626
46552CB00004B/1568